On the Purple Horizon

Poetry

License Notes

Acknowledgments

This book has been a long time coming for me. I just wanted to create a collection of poetry for myself to always be proud of. I feel I have finally accomplished this. Many people have impacted my life before and during the making on this collection; firstly, my incredible parents. My mum and dad have always been hugely supportive throughout every huge downslide, every little hiccup, and every souring moment I have accomplished. I would also like to thank my elder brother Stephen for always being there for me through every experience the poems in this collection are based on and so many more. Another significant person in my life whom I'd like to thank is Justas, my fiancé. He has always supported my dreams since we met and continues to do so daily. Also, his entire family have been hugely supportive! One person I need to thank dearly is my incredible best friend Mari (@poetessofhearts), we actually met on Instagram in the poetry community. She has continued to have a huge impact on my life, and I am incredibly grateful for her presence. Last but far from least my two beautiful children Nate and Lunafreya you two are my entire world!

Contents

On the Purple Horizon

Sunrise

The Key to My Heart

Falling in love

is not an easy thing to do,

for I have to give myself to you,

open up completely,

bring you inside,

instead of locking the door behind me,

I give you a key.

Velvet Lips

The snow landed on
my velvet lips,
freezing my every kiss,
warmth threatening the icy cool,
melting the snow into nothing at all,
moisture is all that remains on my lips,
during these cold snowy days,
pure bliss.

Air

The air,

although invisible,

extremely powerful,

seductive,

necessity.

It's funny we rely on an invisible substance,

yet we're constantly told

don't believe it unless you see it,

how ironic.

We entrust our entire existence on something

we cannot see,

not believing is,

stupidity.

My Universe

You are my universe,

is something you always seem to say,

planets colliding around us,

but together we will be okay,

occasionally hit by asteroids,

sometimes blocking our path,

hand in hand,

we will get past.

Mining into Her Mind

Gazing into her golden eyes,

they flicker in the candlelight,

like a golden nugget in a mining cave,

breath-taking to see,

but to mine for it,

you must be brave,

I watch as she plays with her food,

twirling her fork,

collecting the spaghetti from her plate,

she twists and twirls her hair,

I think something is on her mind.

Do I mine for it?

You

It's you,

it has always been you,

when I awake at sunrise,

it's your face I wish to be greeted by,

your legs draped over mine,

protecting me from the monsters

beneath our bed,

keeping me warm and safe,

until the very end.

Love Struck

Love is a sensational feeling,

the overwhelming feeling of trust,

the horrifying fear of betrayal,

the complete and utter honeymoon period,

the laughs and giggles,

the heart to hearts,

the open mouths,

closed eyes,

skin to skin,

the raw emotion,

the sensational feeling,

it's magnificent,

it's pure,

honest,

true,

no matter how long it lasts,

it will always be you.

Small Downpours

Flowers are most beautiful

when the rain is regular,

but not constant.

When the sun glows brighter,

but not blinding.

Our lives are the same,

we benefit from small downpours,

we shine beneath rays of sunlight,

we go through yearly cycles,

where somethings are

supposed to never change.

The Guard

The leaves blow freely in the wind,

gales battering the branches,

the trunk still standing,

taking responsibility,

fighting against the natural war,

the wind begins to slow,

the leaves, still,

branches left broken,

the trunk has won yet another battle,

the tree survived,

with only a few bruises,

the guard stands tall for another day.

Her

Her beauty

shined like

never before

when she smiled

I just craved

her even more

she made me

happier

than ever

I needed her

In my life

Forever.

The Powerful You

And breathe,

take a deep breath,

sigh,

let out the tension,

let out the vulnerability,

you are strong,

you are powerful,

you are amazing,

preach to yourself,

even if you disagree,

eventually, you will believe,

you will see,

you have a purpose,

you are beautiful,

you are you.

Safe Embrace

You hold my hand,

pulling me closer,

into your warm embrace,

ensuring that I'm safe,

you probably don't realise,

the effect you have on me,

but when you are near,

my body moves,

in the best possible way

I Remember Everything

I remember everything,

even those I wish I could forget,

I remember how the butterflies grew in my

stomach

when you walked into the room,

for the very first time,

I knew you had to be mine,

I remember how your lips felt that night,

we shared our first kiss,

there was no going back from this,

I remember your hands around my waist,

My heart in my throat,

My pulse running, as if it were a race,

My body at that high place,

The best place I've ever been,

I remember all the fights,

all the drama,

all the lonely nights,

it's safe to say we've had good times and bad

but, the good times are the best I've ever
had.

Footprints in My Mind

I smile

every time

you walk

through

my mind.

Leaving only

your delicate

footprints

behind you.

I Have Everything to Lose

Take my hand,

please just take it,

for if you refuse,

I know it's not me you choose,

I have everything to lose,

I won't pretend I don't,

because I do,

I'll lose you,

so please if you truly want me,

show me,

I need to know where I stand,

and which path to take.

Breathe Her In

Breathe her in,

taste every inch of her worthy body,

worship her flaws,

admire her, desire her,

never let her lose hope,

never allow her to feel alone,

for she needs to be shown,

how it feels to be loved,

before she can love herself.

Guardian Angel

If you need it,

you can have it.

You're struggling to breathe?

Take the air right from my chest.

You've cried your last tears?

Here have my tear ducts.

Your heart is broken?

I will love you with all of my heart,

so that yours has time to recover.

Your legs are too weak to carry you any

further?

Jump into my arms.

I can get you where you need to be.

I will always be here to catch you when you

fall.

I will always be your guardian angel.

When She Speaks

Listen to her when she speaks,

she doesn't speak often,

but when she does,

she speaks with all her soul,

so, listen with all of yours,

if you do not,

you will mishear her,

making her feel as if she means

nothing at all.

Kiss My Nose

With tears rolling down my face,

I smile,

pretend everything's okay,

you see through my lies,

take me by the hand,

pull me close,

embrace me tight,

as long as I am in your arms,

I know I will be alright,

so please just stay one more night,

we don't need to do anything,

just hold me,

long enough for my pieces to fit back

together,

sewed perfectly,

ensuring I will not break again,

keep me warm and safe forever on,

wipe my tears away,

kiss my nose,

and smile,

On the Purple Horizon

thank you,

for being a shoulder to cry on.

Unknown Beauty

She could never see
the beauty in herself,
that every other person on the planet
could see.

I Did This for Me

I'm asked if it hurt falling from heaven,

but I didn't fall,

I rose from the depths,

climbed the glass staircase,

out of my misery,

I built myself back up,

brick by brick,

as high as I could reach,

weights tied to my ankles,

not ready to say goodbye,

but I did this for me,

I chose not to hide.

The Second They Meet

Attempting to catch the raindrops,

falling to my feet,

the delicate water droplets,

merging together the second they meet,

reminding me of you?

I Am Worthy

I am worthy,

something I should tell myself more often,

you try to drag me down continuously,

but I am more than that,

I am stronger than that,

I don't belong in the hidden depths far

below,

I am to be known,

my voice has more to say,

than you will ever know,

I will no longer tremble upon the scales,

I will no longer sit in that corner and rock,

Back and forth,

I am worthy,

I am able to look at my broken reflection and

smile,

pull my hair up out of my face,

no longer hiding,

for I am worthy,

I will be okay.

You Don't See It

I hurt sometimes too,

you may not see it,

but I do,

I continue to pick myself up,

battle through the rough,

I refuse to destroy myself,

to save you.

Red Lipstick

Wow, I thought,

every time I lay my eyes on her,

my breath is snatched from my chest,

her long chestnut hair,

caressing her pale face,

her red lipstick on her supple lips,

oh, she takes my breath away,

and her eyes,

her big brown eyes,

pure,

innocent,

stunning,

but, she will never know.

Like A Flower

Like a flower caught in the rain,
your petals won't always remain the same,
so, lean your stem towards the light,
and everything will be just fine.

All I Need

I long for the day when you hold my hand,
because that is what I need from you,
when you pull me close and tell me I have
nothing to fear,
is the day my lungs will be able to breathe
again,
lost in anxiety unable to leave my bed,
drag me out of the comforting duvet and
comfort me instead,
the day my bed is no longer my safe place,
is the day your shoulder becomes it,
my tears soaking your shirt,
instead of my pillow,
revealing to you my over-imaginative mind,
rather than holding it all inside,
that is what I need,
that is what I need from you.

You Still Can

No one said it would be easy,

please don't hide away completely,

let your voice be heard,

teach those that need to learn,

if you allow yourself to run,

you'll be forgotten amongst those who ran,

they never found their strength,

but you still can.

Sleepless Nights

I awake at night,

to the gentle cries,

of my children.

I close my eyes,

and breathe,

I cannot let them see,

the tiredness in me.

I try not to get frustrated,

as my youngest thinks it's playtime,

at the early hour of 3:15.

I hide my exhausted cries,

swear blind that I'm alright,

I'm coping perfectly well,

but sometimes I just need,

a full night's sleep.

One Last Time

My lips mutter your name

under my breath,

over and over again,

until my lungs fully deflate,

unable to inhale,

breathless,

gagging for air,

longing to breathe,

just so I can whisper your name,

one last time.

Nostalgia

In a garden full of memories,

childhood laughter,

playground games,

oh, I remember,

the good old days.

We used to run,

and scream,

as loud as we pleased,

whilst parents,

watched on from a distance.

We would play,

and have fun,

all day long,

until the streetlights

came on,

that's how we knew,

dinner time had come.

Kiss Me Slowly

Kiss me

slowly

don't dare to think

don't dare to blink

your lips melt into mine

savour the taste

let it linger

long enough

until your lips can never

erase the taste of me.

Unwinding of Words

Beauty within the lines,

the happy and sad silent cries,

hiding away so that you don't need to

pretend,

that you're crying into a book,

from beginning to the very end,

the unwinding of words,

helping your mind to unwind,

to clear your head,

to escape from your own life,

even if just for a few seconds,

there is a lot hidden inside,

a lot you don't see at first,

so, breathe,

dig deep,

and believe.

Lost in You

Tracing every inch of you,

with my fingertips,

marking your skin,

with my fingerprints,

it is just us,

it is just us,

alone,

together,

who knows for how long,

maybe, forever?

Daisy Chains

Our love is like a daisy chain,

weaved in every way,

completely interlinked,

beautiful,

fragile,

fairly easy to break.

That's not to say our love is fake,

if one stem does break,

it is also fairly easy to recreate,

we build each other up,

whilst keeping each other safe,

tangled,

hand in hand,

not wanting to escape.

Love can be fiddly,

as well as daisy chains,

you have to connect on a deeper level,

to make it through the breaks.

Last One Standing

The bitter truth hides within those doubtful
eyes,
hiding behind those walls you've built so
high,
finding solitude in a room of empty promises,
no one warned you.
How did you turn out like this?
grab the pickaxe,
bash at your walls,
knock them down,
until the last one standing tall is
you.

Rocks Are Made to be Tough

Our love is like a tidal wave.

I am the wave; you are the rocks.

Continuously crashing into one another.

No matter how bad the damage,

our lips always return to touch,

bodies colliding; much too rough.

It's okay, rocks are made to be tough.

The water splashing up at you,

slapping you in the face.

When the ocean gets angry,

the rocks just sit and wait

for the storm to be over.

Our love is like a tidal wave.

Beautiful, dangerous.

Perfectly safe for us.

Yellow

The yellow sun

rises from beneath

kissing the yellow sand

that lay on the shores

kissing the shore on the cheek

gentle of course

but you can feel the heat

day after day

unsure of what it means.

A Woman Loves

A woman loves

a nice warm bed

a beautiful place

to rest her head.

A woman loves

a faithful mate

someone to take her

on precious dates.

A woman loves

her wonderful children

to build them up

and grow with them.

A woman loves

melted chocolate

to savour the taste

and take her to her happy place.

A woman loves

to read romance

to take her away from reality

when she has no other plans.

On the Purple Horizon

A woman loves

herself

and that's what matters most.

Trust Fall

I need you.

Will you catch me when I fall?

Or drop me in the dirt

as though I'm nothing at all?

Perfume

I smell you.

Your perfume,

this time not on you.

But, on every other girl walking by.

I think I miss you.

No, I do.

If I didn't miss you,

why would every other girl,

smell the way you do?

I may be delusional.

It may all be in my head.

You are always on my mind,

every day,

and every night.

I smell your perfume.

Don't Look Down

Don't look

    D

    O

    W

    N

the fall is harsh

long and painful

keep your head held high

in the clouds

away from those

who drag you

    D

    O

    W

    N

Green

I lay with you,

in a non-sexual way,

gazing into your speckled green eyes,

the eyes that turn the skies

blue from grey,

this is how I know

everything will be okay,

I look deep into your eyes,

I see all your desires,

none of the jealousy or hatred,

only love and purity,

in those,

speckled green eyes.

Always

You are my sunshine

peering through the clouds.

You are my raindrop,

hitting the dry ground,

after a long drought.

You are the blood,

that runs through my veins.

You are the one,

I say I love you to

each and every day.

Sheltered by Your Love

I am completely submerged,

beneath your blanket of love,

safe and warm,

sheltered from above,

if you move,

I will be drowned by the rain,

and all the pain will come flooding in

once again,

you protect me from all that is bad,

you grab me by the hand,

pulling me out of the sinking sand,

and although you drive me crazy,

you are my one and only.

Linger

Laced between your sombre limbs,

tracing my fingertips down your spine,

caressing every inch,

claiming your body, mine,

reaching up to your scarlet lips,

planting a single kiss,

letting it linger for moments,

a few more moments than deemed

innocent.

This Young Girl

A young girl,

not always doing so well,

she laughs,

and she cries,

over thinking every little detail of her

life,

this young girl,

has been through hell and back,

there is a lot she hides,

a lot she keeps hidden,

deep inside,

her heart is no longer pure,

not as pure as before,

she used to be confident,

she used to smile more,

she laughs less now,

even less than before,

but this young girl is strong, and

somehow her battered heart

still beats.

What Matters Most

Happiness is not continuous.

We all have bad days.

What matters most,

is how we spend the happy ones.

Flaws and All

She was the woman I had always dreamt to be,

silk-like hair,

auburn in colour,

resting on the small of her back.

Eyes that always shined,

no matter what was on her mind.

Skin, flawless.

But, no…

I no longer dream to be her.

I am happy with my chestnut hair,

that rests on my shoulders.

I am happy with my hazel eyes,

that only shimmer when I cry.

I am happy in the skin I'm in.

Flaws and all.

What Is Poetry

Poetry is the good and bad,

the misunderstood, the laughed at.

Poetry is the notions I take to make myself

a better person day by day.

Poetry is the heartbreak and sorrow,

the will I see tomorrow.

Poetry is mesmerising for the mind.

Beauty within the lines.

Poetry is the special link in my life.

Sail My Ship

Untie my anchor,

release my ropes,

sail my ship

across the ocean

whilst I'm still

afloat.

I said not today.

Today I shall not

    S

    I

    N

    K

Instead, I shall

ride the waves

despite what you may think.

Forever by Your Side

I hate seeing you like this
when there is nothing I can say.
So, I will give you a big hug,
comfort you and I'll pray for the light
to shine your way.
I promise everything will work out just fine.
You will forever have me by your side.

The Villain in Me

He tilted his head towards you,

offering a twisted smile,

laughing out your name,

he represents all the bad,

that can come with fame,

you try to fight back,

obviously, you lose.

There needs to be a villain,

who has more to prove?

One day you'll see,

that fighting back,

brings out the villain in me.

Warm Fingers

Warm fingers

intertwines with mine

rubbing your thumb around my palm.

Sure enough, I found that this is love.

Sometimes

Sometimes you just need someone to be there.
Listen to your fears.
Understand your reasons.
Someone who isn't too pushy,
but, pushes you inches out of your comfort
zone,
enabling you to walk the yellow brick road
Without prompting.
Someone who will simply hold your hand,
without placing their fingers somewhere else.
Sometimes a hug will do.
Reassurance that you can learn to love you.

12 Word Story

She was stunning.

I studied her every flaw,

loving her even more.

Pointless

You feel pointless.

You can't think of a better word.

You try and try but it's never good enough.

You silently sit alone.

Barely breathing.

Water leaking from your eyes.

You try to think of reasons to carry on,

you can't.

what's the point?

But deep down you know there is a point.

You know it will all work out.

You know the light shines brighter on the

other side.

You know it will just take a while to get

there.

Feeling better and better each day.

Eventually, you will no longer feel

pointless.

You will feel proud and worthy.

Show Me You Love Me

Prove your love for me.

Not by cutting off your arm as a gift.

Kiss my forehead.

Cup my face.

Hold my hand.

Show me you're here to stay.

Right by my side.

Always.

Tears of Joy

Take my tears of sorrow
straight from my ducts
for I no longer wish to cry
over those, I've lost
leave my tears of joy
in place
I will save them for my
happy days.

After I Fall

I rise

again and again

without fail

always

no matter how heavy the hammer

no matter how strong the swing

I fall yes

then I rise

up to my feet

always

ready for the next round

the next round of life

I will always

rise.

Honour Your Calling

Wake up,

everyday,

morning or afternoon,

whatever is best for you,

honour your calling,

stay true to you,

be productive,

or stay in bed,

live your own life,

your life at its best.

Against All Odds

I look up to the skies,

close my eyes and dream,

of all the possibilities,

the probabilities,

the will it ever happen,

whatever the odds,

I continue to dream,

I continue to believe,

that one day,

just maybe,

I will be,

what I've always wanted to be,

as strong as my mother,

as witty as my father,

as brave as my brother,

but still me,

a little warrior,

who never stops,

marching forward.

Only You

No matter how weak

my heart always

continues to beat,

it beats for you.

Poisonous Kisses

Pretty thing,

don't hold your breath.

Speak out,

without doubt,

until you've cleared your pretty head.

Only regret the unsaid.

The words that didn't fall from those lips.

You killed him,

with a single kiss.

Leaving him dreamy,

disorientated,

unable to think freely.

You did this.

No need to be ashamed.

You did this.

It Doesn't Look Good on Me

I'd beg you not to leave

but, this time,

begging doesn't look good on me.

Be Sound

Waking up lost,

missing out,

unknowing of what you've got,

painting on a smile,

fooling everyone, but once in a while,

someone notices,

they see through your makeup,

they look past what you've made up,

offering you a smile, a real one,

and a nice warm hug,

your body slumbers into theirs,

thanking them,

for showing you the life,

you've already won,

look around,

see the world through fresh eyes,

and be sound.

Back to You

I used to believe in superstition,

the fear kept me away from those I love,

the fear kept the space vast between us,

then I woke up,

rode the boisterous waves,

on my broken surfboard,

across the seven seas,

back to you, my love.

Orbit

Planets align

Beings alive

Extra-terrestrial life

Possibilities aside

Here we exist

Side by side

Magnificent rocks

Forming along the dotted line

Rotating perfectly

Orbiting romantically

Always watching

Never touching

The miracle of life we call it

Trust

I trusted you
for only a few moments
that's when I knew I had fallen
completely in love with you.

Beyond Reach

Shimmering in the moonlight,

I stand lakeside,

gazing across the field of water,

the giant tank,

the mystical world,

I wonder what it's like to breathe down

there,

beneath our existence,

in their own huge world,

I realise the world is bigger than just you

and I,

it's filled with many magical worlds,

interlinking yet barely touching,

it's beautiful,

the worlds we cannot reach,

the languages we cannot speak,

the people we cannot meet,

I stand back,

I am living in my world,

I must stay.

Tiptoe Footprints

Treading through the sand,

leaving tiptoe footprint tracks behind me,

marking my imprint on this world.

Irresistible

When in your presence

I come alive

My temperature soars

My heart thrives

My pulse quickens

My mind explodes

My body moves

All on its own

Pulling you closer

Without my consent

Lips parted

Our breathing laboured

You're irresistible

You're intense.

Dandelion Dreams

I closed my eyes

Took a deep breath

Made my wish

And blew.

No Place

You are my safety

When I fall you are my safety net

You catch me before I hit the hard ground

You are my happy

No matter how down

You remove the frown

And replace it with a smile,

You are my home

There is no place like it

You are warm and cosy

My sanctuary

A place I will forever return to.

A Virgin Mother

A fragile life forms,

nestled safely within the lining

of a young woman's womb.

Away from the old-fashioned noise,

of prying eyes and obstinate minds,

already projecting unwanted advice.

Planting landmines

of self-doubt,

bashing down doors,

barging into the room,

where the mother-to-be

is down on her knees,

praying she can stay strong,

until her baby is born.

While walls of confidence

crumble, tumble, to the floor.

Months pass slowly,

labour quickly approaches.

Unforgiving voices hack away at dreams and
hopes.

On the Purple Horizon

Voices of the people she depends upon the
most.

Choices left and right,

difficult to decide.

To be sliced open layer by layer,

or push through an opening centimetres wide?

Drugged up, disorientated, unable to move,

or crying out, begging the pain to subside?

Feeling utterly alone.

Every question has 'that' tone.

The tone we all know.

Her biggest fear?

Answering "wrong", to what,

The "judges" want to hear.

She lies awake most nights in bed,

replaying what they've said,

praying she'll be enough,

for her little legacy of love.

The birth has been and gone,

trailed by a train of expectations,

which, driving full steam ahead,

becomes, relentless.

On the Purple Horizon

Terrified to carry on.

Feeling everything she does,

is wrong

She questions...

"Is a mother's instinct, really that strong?"

"You don't feed your babe by breast?"

"Mummy's homemade milk is better than the rest."

(They don't ever tell her 'fed' is best!)

Teething, crawling, standing, walking,

the first two years were all survived.

She takes a breath and grits her teeth

as cyclone toddler soon arrives.

Kicking and screaming,

screeching loudly,

her child lies on a grimy shop floor.

All the while she is wishing

the ground below,

would swallow her whole.

Her own inner child wants to cry, run and hide.

On the Purple Horizon

Held back by the strength of a warrior
inside.

Followed by the disgusted glares

from shoppers wishing she wasn't there...

She picks up her treasure, fighting back
tears,

a sweet sting of relief as the exit nears,

A slap of fresh air connects with her face,

a hit of realisation.

She tightens her embrace.

Instead of the usual question of why

she wipes her eyes with the sleeve of her
shirt,

Dusts off her crown, leaves her tears in the
dirt.

Looks down at the smile and the bright blue
eyes

and instead of asking the heavens,

She asks herself Why,

Why didn't I see? The only voice, I ever
needed to listen to...

Was me.

Sunset

I Lost Myself

One moment you were there,

and the next you were not,

It's almost as if you've completely forgot,

now you've left me alone,

in this world to rot,

I lost myself in that love of ours,

I wish I didn't need your comforting arms,

but clearly, I do,

subdued,

all thanks to your powerful charms.

One Day

It's dark,

misty,

empty,

I thought,

I knew,

until

one day,

there was

light,

ambition,

love,

happiness,

hope,

the darkness,

the mist,

gone,

the emptiness,

finally, full.

I Hear Them

I hear you,

the words you say under your breath,

I'll never forget,

you say you didn't mean them,

I know you too well,

you say them under your breath,

knowing full well,

this was not going to end well.

Raindrops

The rain is pouring,

hammering on the window,

beckoning me,

welcoming me,

the droplets glisten as they glide down the

glass,

leaving a watery snail trail behind,

the heavens have opened,

unlawfully,

the sad clouds releasing stress,

allowing tears to fall from above,

it drowns us,

creating ocean like features around us,

dragging us under,

camouflaging our own tears,

the clouds taking the blame,

for our own fears.

Are You Happier Now?

Are you happier now?

I hate to think that you are,

it hurts,

it hurts so damn bad,

you were the best I ever had,

I begged you to stay,

how stupid of me,

you still walked away,

I promised myself,

I will never make that same mistake.

The Damage Was Done

Lying on the ground,

this time around,

I was too weak to make a stand,

images flashing through my mind,

every little thing,

replaying over and over,

I hide,

I hide and I cry,

I cry till my eyes bleed,

bleed till they run dry,

evil words they fired from their lips,

then walking away,

looking back for a second glimpse,

making sure this time,

the damage was done,

my body a tomb for the girl I once was,

decaying over time as no one came to look,

although I have healed on the outside,

my insides will always be scarred,

these memories will never leave my side,

On the Purple Horizon

but I am thankful that I left you out of my
life.

Change

Change,

I struggle with the word,

it frightens me,

I prefer structure and routine,

change does not sit well with me,

I know change can be good,

I know it takes time to adjust,

but sometimes,

change is simply too much.

Missing Piece

What the hell am I supposed to do,

now that I no longer have you,

you are the missing piece of my puzzle,

the one piece I can't seem to find,

frustrated,

saddened in disguise,

how can I complete my puzzle,

with a space that remains empty?

that, you cannot expect of me,

If you hear my inner cries,

please rush back by my side,

I need you more than I thought I did,

I need you in my life.

Frozen Heart

You froze my heart.

Left me in the dark.

Turning my skin that

pale shade of blue.

Leaving me more fragile

than ever before.

I Set Her Free

I spat evil words at her,

as though she meant nothing,

I made her feel unworthy,

in reality, she was too good for me,

I made my voice loud,

to seem superior,

to keep her bound,

I scared her,

yet she still stuck around,

she could never find a fault,

she would give me my own excuses,

blaming herself,

knowing it was all on me,

time and time again,

look at what I've done,

I destroyed her,

a burden I cannot bear,

tomorrow she will awake,

for me not to be there,

she will be sad at first,

On the Purple Horizon

but one day she will see,

I didn't leave to hurt her,

I left to set her free.

Unfixable

I don't expect you to be able to fix it.

It's not something that can be fixed.

Just stand by me, and hold me tight,

this time it will not be all alright,

so, allow me to cry,

allow me to fight,

allow me to scream and shout,

I need to get it all out,

unjudged, without doubt.

Bad Dreams

Does it hurt
when you lay
awake at night.

Are you haunted
by your dreams?
are you sure
that you're alright?

The twisted reality
can seem like
dreams sometimes.

No not dreams
the bad ones
that never allow
you to sleep.

Nightmares
they call them.

Acceptance

Drowning in the depths of despair,

it's okay, there is no need to be scared,

there is no need to struggle,

no need to fight,

this is one of those moments,

where you allow your body to take flight,

this is not giving up,

this is choosing to accept what is left to

come.

Passing Moments

Every so often,

the moon and the sun,

their fingertips touch,

touch for seconds,

as the moment passes,

once in a while,

the sun and the moon,

come face to face,

just briefly,

as the orbit continues,

occasionally,

we meet our soul mates,

in the wrong moment,

or maybe it was so right,

that it just wasn't supposed

to last very long.

A Cut Too Deep

Bright blue blood

R

  U

    N

     N

      I

       N

        G

Through my veins

The only substance

Keeping me safe and sound

If you cut deep enough

The blood leaks out

Dripping

Bright red blood.

Lingering Pain

There is an ache inside my head

Claiming me his home

I try to throw him out

But he has made my head his own

My heart is wilting

Tears draining all the moisture

There will soon be nothing left

My body already so fragile

You come and push me over the edge

My eyes are so sore

From glaring into your empty promises

I believe every word that falls from

Your dangerous lips

Dangerous because somehow

You manage to solve all this

With one gentle kiss

You can make me or break me

With a snap of your fingers

You break me so many times

That when you make me the pain still lingers

On the Purple Horizon

What hurts the most

Is the love I have for you

Now I'm drowning in your love

And I don't know what to do

Maybe I need some help

But I don't think I want any help from you

Faded Dreams

What once were so colourful
Now only screen in black and white
Dreams filled with joy and laughter
Now abandoned with no light in sight
The nightmares have taken over
Removing all happiness from my sleep
Faded dreams set out to destroy me
Rewarded by silent screams.

Why Me?

Why did you choose me?

You claimed my body as your own

Why can I not just let it go?

I remember that night so vividly

I remember the look in your eye

When I said no

I watched the anger pile up inside

Why did I not run or scream?

Maybe because I didn't have enough fight left

in me

so, you won

you can brag and act proud

I hope you always remember

No, it wasn't fun

I really wish I could let go

But how can I let go

When I still don't know

Why me?

Late Nights

Cloudy mind on this late night

Unable to fall asleep

Fireworks inside my head

Refusing to let me be

Bang bang pop

My head explodes

Will these thoughts

Ever leave me alone?

The Mirror Lied

The mirror lied

Her hips were not that wide

Her thighs were not that thick

This is what her reflection would spit

The curse of the broken girl

Relying on her reflection to make her look

Well

How sad she must be

The only thing telling her how bad she must

Be

Is an object

Made of glass

Hung on the wall

The least trustworthy object of all

Tarnished Souls

Beaten and bruised

Nothing more to lose

Collapsed onto the ground

Too defeated to take a stand

Nothing left to say

You left my soul tarnished

By your demonic ways

Please, Keep It

Each and every one of my organs are failing

My mental state derailing

Don't you see

I can no longer breathe for myself

I need you to breathe for me

This isn't how I wanted us to end

This is how God wanted it to be

I am ever so sorry

I never planned to leave you behind

I realise now

Life isn't always kind

But the day I was given you

You took my breath away

So, please

Keep it

You see I no longer need it

Every breath you continue to make

Means my memory is still in place

Immoral Ideation

Look at you

With your immoral ideation

Burning inside of you

Like a hideous infestation

Completely out ruling your moral side

Is it really that hard just to be kind

Silent Cries

There is a doll

Sat in the corner

Of the room

Making eye contact

With everyone who

Comes into view

Sometimes at night

You can hear her

Silent cries

Porcelain lips

Unable to move

She sits and weeps

There is sadness in her eyes

She was left behind

When she died

Favourite Drink

You stole a sip

From your favourite drink

To fulfil your deadly thirst

It just so happened to be

That your favourite drink

Was me

Burned Flesh

Chains

Strapped to my

Chest

Weighing me down

I shall never

Forget

Flesh forever scarred

Burned

Charred

Marked memories

Still sting the sores

From the night

I was reborn

Why Couldn't You See?

She was stunning

Why couldn't you see?

You left running

She was stunning

You were cunning

You kept her under lock and key

She was stunning

Why couldn't you see?

Shallow

You found me

Pulled me out

From under the dirt

Brushed me off and

Held my hand

Stood by me through everything

Even when it was

Never your plan

You were hurting inside

I could always tell

I would be there for you

And protect you from it all

Yet it was never

Never enough

You continued to fall

You continued to drown yourself

I was the lifeguard

Dragging you back to the surface

Saving you from yourself

You loved me with all your heart

On the Purple Horizon

You loved me way too much

You thought you were saving me

Yet I was the one left alone and hurt

What you thought was a selfless act

Had selfish consequences

You just didn't stick around to see

Never Forgotten

I hated you

Trembled in the presence of a friend

By pure free will, I escaped your embrace

All memory of you left in the past

But never forgotten

I Did Scream

I screamed

I know I did

But you could not hear me

No one could hear me

My silent screams

Echoed in my brain

Unable to get out

My mouth opened

But my throat remained shut

Refusing to let out my fear

I needed to scream

I swear I did

But my lungs closed up

I did scream

Hours Lost

It's such a shame

The time we missed out on

The minutes

The hours

The days

Lost

I wish we could have had more time

But sadly we cannot

Actions Speak Louder

You held me in the palm of your hand

Clenched your fist tight

Grounding me down to dust

Destroying every piece of me with one touch

The worst of it is

You would not be able to remember

What your hands have done

I always will

I will never be able to move on

Actions speak louder than words

They say

You proved this theory correct

With what you did that day

For what you've done rings louder in my head

Than the words that fall from your tongue

Young and Dumb

I was too blind to see

I was pushing you away from me

I was young and dumb

I am so sorry that

You lost yourself when

You lost me

Left to Dry

If I say

I'm not okay

I am begging for you to listen

Please

Do not scoff or

Chuckle under your breath

Do not tell me what is best

Just hold my hand

And hug me tight

Just long enough for

The glue to dry

So, I can convince myself

That I will be alright

Deadly Thoughts

I lay my head

On a bed of roses

Soaking the petals

With my tears

Imagining my worst fears

Witling the flowers

With my deadly thoughts

Not intentionally of course

Their Game

Someone is inside my head

I do not think they want to be friends

They scream at me a lot

They tell me I am not enough

So I just sit and listen

Lured into their every word

Trapped in my fractured skull

The key I swallowed was my only escape

That thing in my head

Wanted it to be this way

They enjoy playing this evil game

A game I am forever subjected to

A game where you cannot win or lose

There is nothing to prove

I will bow my head in shame

Whilst I continue playing their game

Suspended Above

Hanging by a thread

Tied around my neck

Suspended above

All those I love

My head completely full of regret

Too many things left unsaid

But

It's too late

The deal with the devil is done

My name is signed on that dotted line

Continuously Pushing

You do make me happy I cry

I know I may complain

But I do try

I'm trying to tell you

Honestly how I feel

Somehow to you, it doesn't seem real

What more can I do

To make you believe me

You think I don't love you

As much as before

I laugh it off tell you to trust me

Yet you continue to push

More and more

We are up all night

With our continuous fights

Can you honestly tell me

Everything will be alright

If I just keep my mouth shut

On the Purple Horizon

Then maybe it might.

Just Sixteen

You hurt me

When I was just sixteen years old

I thought my whole world had fallen apart

Oh how was I so wrong

Hurting so young wasn't any fun

But I learnt from your mistakes

From your fake precious lies

From your too good to be true kind eyes

You made me realise

Ups and Downs

Sometimes you scare me

You shout so loud

You make my body completely freeze

Sometimes you drown me

Ignoring my thoughts

Only focusing on your own

Sometimes you upset me

Leaving me alone

In my bed all night long

Mostly you get me

We harmonise like a song

Mostly you praise me

And listen to me

When I tell you what is wrong

Mostly you love me

Keeping me warm and safe

Embracing me from the moment we fall asleep

Until the first light of dawn

Beware

I was so mislead

Easy dreaming

Pool water gleaming

Tempting to you take the dive

Jump off the cliff of life

Ps.

Beware of the rocks

Earthquake

The silence is so loud

Booming through the house

I thought I knew what empty felt like

I guess…

I was wrong…

I didn't know at all

The silence made the ground shake

Framed photos fell from the walls

Doors fell from their hinges

An earthquake had hit

One silent earthquake

Main Meal

You eat away

Blood drooling down

You wipe your lips

With the back of your hand

I see you lick your lips

No regret

Not an inch of self-doubt

You eat away

As though you cannot live without

A Victim of Love Loss

I fall

Through your heart

You missed out

On your only chance

All you felt

Was a small

Palpitation

That lasted

Mealy moments

Not long enough to notice

I am the victim of

Love loss

Heartbroken

By the boy

Who let me slip

Through his

Fingers

Healing

I loved you

When you were broken

Helped you heal

You couldn't love me

Because I was too broken

I understood that

Let you go

Left to heal alone

Shattered Heart

Some days it's almost impossible to move on

A day in bed watching a rom-com

Stuffing your face

With your favourite ice-cream

Sobbing uncontrollably

And yet

Some days your heart is strong

Strings reattaching piece by piece

Helping your heart to move on

Always remaining torn

I Never Did Find My Escape

Staring through the window at night

Although not really looking through the glass

More like gazing into my reality filled

Reflection

Unable to break eye contact

Relentlessly trying to look away

I never did find my escape

Taken Moments

You took a moment that mattered

You took away my innocence

Leaving behind insecurity

You gave yourself that power

A taken moment I can never replace

A taken moment I can never reclaim

Thank god

I had the strength to stop you

From taking any-more of my moments

Disconnected

The words don't fall from my mouth

No matter how hard I try to spit them out

There is so much to say

Yet it feels like my lips like to disobey

My tongue rolling forming words

Still, no sound to be heard

Throat aching begging to be heard

Still… nothing

Midnight Kisses

I kissed the moon goodnight

Lingered for longer than I should have

I wasn't ready to say goodbye

I wasn't ready to be lost in the night

Far away from any beacon of light

To show me the way

So, I cradled the moon

As though I were a babe

Clinging to my mother's breast

Refusing to be removed

Frightened of letting go

I continued to say no

And held on for as long as I possibly could

Until my limbs grew numb

And my eyes drew closed

It Sure Is Painful

Ever heard of love loss?
You either lose someone you love
Or lose all love for yourself
I don't know which one hurts more

Rewired

I am a very controlling person

I like things done my way

It's not like I can help it

I don't try to be this way

I wake up every day hoping the wires in my

Brain may have been rearranged

But that is never the case

Even if I try to rewire myself

It always goes wrong

It simply cannot be done

At least as of yet

Above all I am scared

Scared of the changes

The changes I believe I want to make

Yet I am unsure if my personality is at stake

I'm not setting out to change myself

At least that was never my intention

I just wanted to fix the controlling side

That everyone seems to strongly dislike

Light and Dark

The darkness seems as though it will stay

Whilst I'm left wishing it will go away

Hope gets me through the day

Praying for the light to shine my way

I need the goodness to scare off the bad

I need the light life I've always wished to

Have

Keep My Eyes

I fell so deeply in love

Much too fast

You stole my eyes

Love made me blind

I took a knife

Slit through the curtains

The curtains smothering me

Whilst I slept

Whilst I wept

Easing the knife through the fabric

Wishing it were your throat

Keep my eyes

I don't need them

I screamed

For I never want to love again

I never want to bleed

Frosted Glass

Her eyes

Glazed over

Almost like

Peering through

Frosted glass

She knew

Their love

Could never

Last

Not Today

The sun rose

Way too early

No earlier than usual

But today

I pretended not to see the sun

I wished for the moon's return

I prayed for daylight not to come

Pulling the duvet over my head

Until I could no longer ignore

The beams seeping through the glass

Until the rays shone too bright

For my sombre state to last

Torn to Shreds

You hurt me

You ripped open my chest

Stole my fragile heart

And left

Thick Black

Open your eyes

Go on look outside

Devour the air

Enjoy it my friend

For one day

It will all come to an end

Our lungs will collapse

Our last breath will escape our parted mouths

Our eyes will roll back

And black

Only thick black

On the Purple Horizon

The Struggle

When I am already struggling

To save myself

How do you expect me

To save you

Rose

The beauty is undeniable

Pure and innocent

A true artistic creation

A gift to the human eye

The rain leaves droplets of water

On the fine petals

Too heavy for the silk-like texture

We cut it

We take the beautiful rose home

Place it in a glass half full

The happiness fades

The petals droop

The colour runs

The red is now inked brown

Tilted

Saddened

We suffocated it

We took the beauty away

We killed it

We took advantage

It Burns

The fire inside

Burning so harshly

It is a shame you cannot see

What you are doing to me

I'm Okay

Door slams

I scream

Not from pain

From anger

The river begins to flow

The unwelcome stream

Puddles evolve around me

I collapse onto my knees

Attempting to catch the river

Running between my fingers

Glazing over my cheeks

My shirt wet

Tear stained Pokka dots

I wipe my eyes

Gather myself

Breathe deeply

And smile

I'm okay

Whipping Wind

You appear on the coldest of days

Scaring away the rays of the sun

Howling at the trees

The branches shiver with fear

I can see that you are near

You are the whipping winds

That comes with a storm

Save Me from My Fate

Drowned by the unknown

Choked by the hatred

Hands wrapped tightly

Around my throat

Dragging me further

Into that place I dare not go

I prayed for escape

Interlinking my fragile fingers

Raising them to my chest

I prayed for so long

With no apparent answer

Where was he when I needed him most

He left me on this earth to starve

He left my body to roast

I continue to wait hoping

Someday he will hear my prayers

And save me from my fate

That Call

Waiting is the hardest thing you could ever
do

Waiting to hear if the news is bad or good

Waiting for that one call that could

Turn your life spinning out of control

I don't want to wait anymore

Posh Princess

Give my mind a rest

Allow me to think and build our nest

I know I'm no better than anyone else

Through I have to try, try to better myself

I refuse to watch the world pass by

Without taking every opportunity that comes
my way

Learning everywhere I can

Even without your supportive hand

Posh princess, you once called me

For choosing to better myself and study

But can you blame me I just want the best for
our kids

For once I am doing something that makes me
feel like I exist

You continue pushing

As if I'll stay by default

The world does not work like that

If I must I will walk out

You take me for granted

Lacking great fear

On the Purple Horizon

As one day you'll find

I'll no longer be there

Is This Any Different

Do you love me

Like you loved her

Or are we different?

Evil Minds

Bent knees

Crouched down

Beside my bed

Praying for forgiveness

Begging for redemption

Joints weak

From an old injury

Will I ever be clean

I need a place to hide

Will evil ever leave my side

I hide away from my psychopathic twisted mind

The mind I used to believe was safe

The mind I thought helped me through my dark days

Not as Broken as You Hoped

Eventually

I forgot about you

I guess I wasn't as broken

As you thought

Why Did You Have to Die?

We forever stand

Side by side

Even after we said

Our last goodbye

If I ever felt alone

You were the one

I could always call home

You were there

To catch me when I fell

Now I hit the concrete

You're not here at all

You said

You'd never leave me

Why did you have to lie

You told me you would

Always be my side

Why did you have to die

Everything... Was Never Enough

I gave everything I had to you
All you felt was a slight palpitation

The Skeleton Left of Me

I feel sick

I'm hungry yet I refuse to eat

I pull every part of me apart

Until I am no longer complete

I am defeated

I have grown too weak

I try so hard to get back up

But I cannot steady my feet

My wobbly knees no longer able to support

The skeleton left of me

I am sick

Drowned by this illness

Smothering me whilst I sleep

How can I escape whilst paralyzed in my wake

Is this my fate

Am I truly awake

Because if this is just a dream

Please someone come and save me

Am I Dead?

Screaming

Without sound

Heart hits the ground

Am I dead?

Mirror Talk

I walked away

Away from what I loved the most

Most of all it killed me

Me myself and I all alone

Alone in this busy world trying to get by

Trying, to find myself once again

I cannot pretend no more

This was the hardest choice of all

Of all the choices I've ever faced, I've ever made

This one, this one was tough

Because I left the one I love, I left you

I Always looked back

Back into your eyes, the ones I left destroyed

I saw the sadness and despair

And I promise you I really do care

But it wasn't fair on me, staying wasn't fair on us

We hit self-destruct that big red button we dared not to touch

So what went wrong?

On the Purple Horizon

Was it that your favorite song was no longer
my favorite song?

Was it the one-sided conversations or the
regular arguments

Everything used to be so grand

We would walk around town holding hands

You treated me like your goddess

It's like you forget about that part

The parts where you showed me you cared

You kissed my forehead and lingered

As if you were scared of letting go

I guess you got too comfortable as that fear
left your mind

You forgot that I was semi-permanent easy to
wash out

Eventually, you washed me out of your life

And preferred it that way, but then I was
gone

You're alone and afraid guilty of the choice
you made

I'm so sorry for your regret but you did this
to yourself

So when you ask what went wrong, look in the
mirror

And while you're at it find a new favorite
song

On the Purple Horizon

On the Purple Horizon

Thank you for reading

24353601R00104

Printed in Great Britain
by Amazon